Story # 1: The New Orleans Crime Boss

CHAPTER 1

As she sexily slithered out of her private limousine in front of the swanky hotel, Alex couldn't take his eyes off her. Her legs were long and dark, and they matched the silky dress she was wearing. She was stunningly beautiful throughout all facets of her physical being. Not only was her body extremely well built,

Three Short Stories of Romance, Mystery, and Intrigue

By Hank Roberts

Story by Hank Roberts

© Hank Roberts 2022

All Rights Reserved

Published by Doctor's Dreams Publishing

PO Box 4808

Biloxi, MS 39535

www.Doctors-Dreams.com

Prepared in the United States of America

ISBN: 978-1-942181-29-3

but her face also shone like diamonds on a gorgeous necklace. Streaming black hair which curled sensuously around her face and down her back was a lovely addition to her total appearance. Alex was surprised to see that her lipstick and her fingernails were not painted bright red. They were a soft pink, which only added intrigue to her very nature. As she strolled to the check-in counter, every muscle of her legs and buttocks protruded through the fine material of her dress. One would think that she had just been introduced at the Oscars.

At the check in desk, she took out her credit card and identification. It was easy for Alex to see that she had reservations for her stay and the entire hotel staff were prepared for her arrival. A bellman hurried to her limousine and gathered her two name-brand luggage pieces. He obviously knew where she was to stay because he immediately disappeared to deliver her bags to her room. Everything seemed to be well organized and meticulously carried out. There was no question that this lady was one of importance, both to herself and to those who had arranged for her trip here to the large city.

The lady strolled to the elevator, accompanied by the manager of the hotel. As she entered the elevator the manager told her to feel free to call upon him if she had any needs or requests.

Alex Trenton, being the top-ranking officer in the local district FBI, knew well what this fair lady was doing in his jurisdiction. He only wished he could get closer to her and find out all the details of her visit. He knew that her name was Karen Karrigan and that she was the mistress of one of the highest kingpins in the nation's underworld. Alex had been tipped off as to her arrival, but he wasn't sure of her intentions in the city. New Orleans has its share of Crime bosses, but the FBI is only called in when a crime, or potential crime, affects the welfare of the United States. It was Alex's thought that Karen must be here for some sort of illegal international activity. New Orleans could easily be accessed by land, water, and air. There was an international airport, as well as an international ship port. Interstate highway I-10 goes from California to the east coast, directly through New Orleans. Drug and human trafficking were a common occurrence through these busy entries into the city.

Alex had two major questions that had to be answered. What was the reason for the mob to be represented here by this high-ranking person and what was the mob's planned activity? The only way that Alex could figure out the answers that he needed was to try to get close to Karen, which was a difficult and dangerous task. Surely Miss Karrigan would have watchmen closely observing her activities and every move. Her being the mistress of one of the mob bosses didn't make the task any easier.

Upon close observation, Alex discovered that Karen took her evening meal there at the hotel restaurant, the Lovers Dream, which was very well known and accepted as a leading restaurant in the city. She had also had a small bottle of Crown Royal delivered to her room each evening. In the hotel housekeepers' dirty linen bag, Alex found a partially consumed empty bottle of the Crown Royal that Karen had ordered to her room the night before. This showed him that his mystery woman was not an alcoholic but rather a moderate drinker. All these observations assisted Alex in his research of the upcoming illegal activity.

It was a well acknowledged fact that Karen Karrigan was not only the close acquaintance of the mob boss, Franko Delito, she was, herself, a skilled con lady and a successful jewel thief. It was said that over the years Karen had accumulated several million dollars of illegal jewels. Because of her association with the underworld, it had been virtually impossible to track down and seize any of her ill gained bounty.

Every evening, 30 minutes before or after Karen arrived at the Lovers Dream restaurant, Alex would come in and take a seat at the bar. He would always order a Crown and water, light on the Crown. It was served in a tall ice filled glass. He never finished his cocktail but his drinking on it always provided time for him to gain information about the beautiful lady in question. Alex studied Karen's every movement, her eating habits and with whom she kept company. He would feed back all this information to his home office where his assistants compiled a complete diary for Alex's for later consideration.

After 4 or 5 evenings of dining experiences, Ms. Karrigan noticed that Alex was always present. He didn't seem to pay much attention to her, but she noticed that he was always there. Karen, being the observant person that she was, noticed that Alex would always order her favorite bourbon. He would always take it with water on the rocks. Alex ordered his drink just like she enjoyed her drinks.

She wandered over to the bar and asked if she could have a seat next to him. Her appearance made it a certainty that she would not be rejected. As soon as Karen introduced herself, under a false name, Alex inquired of her if she was a prostitute. Hookers often hung out in ritzy establishments trying to pick up wealthy marks, or clients. Karen was rather taken back by the blunt question. She assured him that she was in no such profession and only came over because she noticed that he was drinking the same drink that she drank. Alex apologized for his bold question to her. He told Karen that all the lovely ladies that he had met in the city were all prostitutes.

They had no interest in him, only his money. They both had a laugh over the situation and continued with their conversation.

"Are you in New Orleans for business or for pleasure?" inquired the FBI agent, as if he didn't already know.

Karen said that she was there for a clothing buyers' meeting. "This is one of the best locations for a clothier to come and purchase their ware. What is the reason for your visit to the Cajun capital of the world?"

"I own a large fine restaurant in New Mexico, and I am here to try to steal a great chef away from one of the local establishments. Fine food is only as great as the one who prepares it, and it is only as fine as the establishment that serves it."

"You seem like a very pleasant gentleman," said Karen. "Would you like to join me tomorrow at my table for dinner?"

What great luck. Alex was getting closer to Karen and quicker than he had ever imagined. He would need to remain quite secretive and properly play his hand as an undercover FBI agent to the fullest. The agent went back to his room and contacted his office crew with all the new information. They must furnish him with an alibi for his restaurant in New Mexico, as well as bring him up to date on all that was to be known about owning such a business. The next morning Alex checked at the front desk and found a packet that contained a New Mexico driver's license, as well as extensive information concerning the ownership and running of a fine restaurant.

Alex noticed, as he was leaving the hotel, that Karen was getting into a taxi right outside of the lobby. He got the numbers off the cab and called it in to find out what his people knew about it. They said that the taxi in question was assigned to the area of the lower 9th ward of the city. There was really no reason for it, or the driver, to be in this swanky part of town. What were they doing there and what business did they have with Ms. Karrigan? Alex found that the driver's name was Rocky, and he was affiliated with a lowlife mobster in that section of New Orleans. The 9th ward was known for its criminal faction, as well as the criminals who lived there and skirted the law at every chance they got. It was found that Rocky's boss was none other than George de Garos, one of the kingpins of the 9th ward mafia. He was nowhere as big, or as important, as he thought he was, but he still got away with numerous petty criminal offenses. The police of his ward were all in his back pocket. They would provide favors for each other, such as free tickets to the football games in exchange for turning their backson his petty offenses. Although he was a lowlife, he never had to spend a night in jail, and he never paid any of his traffic tickets. He just skirted around their community doing his criminal work and taking advantage of the less fortunate people who lived in that area. George could never be pinned down to any activity of human trafficking or smuggling, however he was often accused of such activities. Could he be a part of whatever activity Karen had been sent here for? Since the 9th ward was adjacent to the Mississippi River, Alex decided that he would focus his investigations on illegal activities that took place on, or near, the water.

That afternoon Alex was picked up by an unmarked FBI car and taken to the residence of George de Garos in the lower 9th ward. Alex found that

George lived in a large, gated compound which housed several apartments, a swimming pool, a garden, and a tennis court. The compound was encircled with extremely low rent housing and residents of little means. Basically, it was an oasis in the middle of this poverty desert. When he stopped to question some of the local residents, Alex was always greeted with the highest of praise for their neighbor George. It seemed that George had bought appliances and food items, as well as medical supplies, for his needy neighbors in order to keep their silence and dedication. No one knew of any criminal activity with which George was affiliated. They just kept their mouth shut and the gifts coming in.

Chapter 2

Alex called his trusted sidekick, Milton, and asked him to do some investigation into the activities of George de Garos. The man had no obvious means of supporting himself, however, he drove a fancy new automobile and he lived in a very nice, fenced complex. Something was very fishy, and it wasn't just because they were close to the river.

Milt immediately got to work finding out all he could about Mr. Garos. The New Orleans FBI office was also very happy to pitch in and see if they could find anything about this shady character.

"While you are at it," said Alex, "get all of the information that you can on a Ms. Karen Karrigan. Who are her friends here in New Orleans, what are her likes and dislikes, who does she hang with, and most of all, what is she doing this far south? I'll meet you this evening at Geno's, a small bar in the French quarter. We'll have a drink and go over what you have found."

That evening, Milton and Alexander met at Geno's, as planned. Milton told Alex that he had some very interesting news for him that he dug up while he was looking for information about George and Karen.

"Karen is the mistress of one Franko Delito, a high-ranking mobster from Boston,", started Milt. "He and Karen live in different cities and did not get a chance to visit often. It's a known fact that Karen likes to entertain other rich and handsome gentlemen. She tries to keep her affairs covered up so Franko won't find out."

"What if Mr. Delito did find out about her escapades?" asked Alex.

"Well," said Milt, "none of the men were ever harmed, physically. On one occasion when Delito found out about an affair that Karen had, he picked her up in his limousine, had his tough guys beat her to within an inch of her life, stripped her of all but her panties and bra, and dropped her off in the middle of Boston so others could see what happened to people that went against Franko. No one had the kahunas to assist Karen or to even give her a lift to a hospital. They knew what Franko would do to them."

It appeared that Franko Delito simply wanted to keep Karen for a trophy girlfriend. He really wasn't interested in her physical welfare. He did, however, have an eye on the many diamonds that Karen had stolen. No one, including Delito, knew where she kept the ill-gotten diamonds. Perhaps her keeping the jewels was as safe a place as anywhere. Franko knew that Karen would guard them with her life and that was all right with him.

Milton continued with telling Alex about his legal findings. "We uncovered the fact that George de Goros is a first cousin to Franko Delito. Delito set him up in New Orleans and provided him with many underworld contacts. George was put on the board of directors of one of the local colleges. He was also recognized by the city for having contributed to many charity organizations. No wonder so many people liked George, even if it was for non-ethical reasons."

One of George's major jobs for the mob was to arrange for smuggling of items, especially cocaine, into the

States through shipping traffic on the Mississippi River. George had several contacts with seafood importers and could easily receive shipments disguised as frozen shrimp or fish. One of George's special inventions was a Tupperware type container which was used to store the cocaine. The container was then frozen and surrounded by a layer of seafood. The smell of the seafood surrounding all sides of the cocaine container made it impossible for drug dogs or import officials to detect the shipment. As all good crook stories go, this idea didn't last long. When the officials began xraying the containers, a strange void was found to be within the seafood. Busted.

Alex inquired, "Do you have any idea how Karen and George are tied up, and what evil scheme are they planning?"

"I don't have any idea, but I am having a team from the agency go down and keep an eye on all the ships that are coming in that have any connection with George. I don't think George is bright enough to arrange trafficking of anything on a large scale. He may, however, be arranging for the shipments on the ships coming into the New Orleans port. Let's both keep our eyes peeled."

That evening Alex again went to the Lovers Dream restaurant, where he saw Karen Karrigan. Since they had met earlier, Alex went over to Karen's table and asked if he could join her.

"Would you mind having dinner with a rich, handsome, and charming restaurateur?" Alex queried. "I hate to be so bold, but I think that I have found the ideal chef for my restaurant. I was so happy that I just wanted someone to share it with."

"Sit right down," Karen replied. "I have also gotten some good news from the people that I am working with here in the city. Perhaps it would be more difficult for me to explain my business than for you."

"Maybe after a fine dinner and some splendid wine, we could retire to your room and have another nightcap," said Alex.

"That sounds like a splendid idea," Karen replied. "After all, I do like rich handsome gentlemen. Maybe you will even find it desirable to spend the night."

Wow. What had he gotten into? Maybe the first part of this plan would be an ideal way to coax some information out of his friend before she got too drunk and fell asleep. Who knows? I'll have to play this hand very carefully and intelligently, thought our FBI agent.

Up in her room, Karen and Alex felt more private and intimate. "Make yourself at home and I will go into the other room and slip on something more comfortable," Karen said. "Just throw your jacket over the chair and I will be back in a jiffy." Karen proceeded to the other room to change her clothes while

Alex turned on some soft music on the radio. When Ms. Karrigan returned, she was dressed in a lovely nightgown that flowed down to the floor. It was completely see-through, and Alex could easily see the lovely panties that she was wearing.

"Does this outfit meet with your approval," queried Karen in a seductive voice.

Agent Trenton had to take a big breath and then swallow. He couldn't remember when he had seen such a beautiful woman, especially one that was scantly clothed.

"Not meaning to be trite but you are the loveliest thing that I have ever seen," said Alex.

"Let me fix you a drink," said Karen, "and let's get more comfortable."

I thought that this was the man's line, thought the shy FBI agent. He cocked back on a reclining couch and waited for his newly poured cocktail. When Karen brought the drink over to Alex, she sat down on his lap and cuddled up to his neck.

This is going to be harder than I thought, thought Alex. He didn't refuse the attention and soon they both were enjoying each other's company.

"Do you have any special friends here in New Orleans?" Alex asked.

"Not really. I am pretty much a loner. I feel much more comfortable in the company of a gentleman than with another woman," was Karen's reply. "I do have a boyfriend back home, but we are not really close. I don't mind admitting that I enjoy spending time with other men. You are the one on my mind presently."

After the drinks had been flowing for a while, Alex began to feel that he could question Karen about some of her activities.

"Besides attending the clothing meetings, what do you do in the city with your spare time," Alexander asked, hoping she would reveal some of her underworld plans.

"Oh, I'm here on a twofold mission. I want to see to some of my Boston boyfriend's import business and I want to arrange for some export of my own. I have a small collection of jewelry that I am planning to sell to a friend in Brazil. It isn't very much but he really wants it and I plan to sell it to him."

"What about your boyfriend's import business? Are there some items that he plans to receive here in New Orleans?" Mr. Trenton inquired. "Oh, never mind. I don't want for you to think that I am delving into your private business."

"You can discuss with me anything that you feel comfortable with. I'm just here for pleasure and relaxation."

Ms. Karrigan spoke up and said, "I have never felt as comfortable with any other man. I love the way you run your fingers through my hair, and I love the touch of your soft hands on my body. It's strange, but I feel that I can discuss anything with you. I just don't want to bore you with my silly business affairs. Most men that I meet are interested in only one thing. You seem to be really interested in me, as a lady."

Alex relaxed into the arms of this lovely woman. Was he dreaming or was this true? He asked her if they could start with small things and then work up.

She said, "Okay. Let's start with my boyfriend's business deals. I really want to get that matter off my mind. He only uses me for his own profits, when and where I am needed. Now he wants me to seduce a ship captain and get him to agree to transfer some illegal drugs from here to Miami. He puts me in all the dangerous positions while he rakes in all the profits. I don't want to seduce a captain. I want to be in your tender arms. I would rat him out except for the fact that he would know and come after me."

"I have a great idea," was Alex's reply. "I will go with you to the ship, and I will deal with the captain. I only have a couple of questions. Who will be arranging for the ship and when will the drugs be delivered to New Orleans to be put on the ship."

Karen paused for a second and then she replied, "I have a friend in New Orleans that is related to my boyfriend. He lives in the 9th ward of the city, and he will make arrangements for the ship. The New Orleans friend, George de Garos, has his own compound down by the river. He has no, or not much, interference from the local police. No one goes onto George's property without his consent. There are large storage rooms there where he stores the drugs. Often these storage rooms are disguised as apartments.

There is also a large storage room under the tennis court. The drugs came into the city several days ago, but he is having a hard time convincing any of the captains to transport them out of the city and down the river."

Wow. This was one half of all Alex needed to know. Like a true gentleman, he assured Karen that her secrets were safe with him.

"Let's settle back on the bed and enjoy some late night adult entertainment," said Alex. "We will work out all the details tomorrow when we wake up. Now it's time for us to become closer friends."

Chapter 3

The very next morning, as soon as the couple got out of bed, Alex suggested that he go to his room to tidy up and dress for breakfast. He suggested that they had a lot of planning to do but they could plan all of this at their morning restaurant rendezvous. Karen was pleased with these arrangements and set a time for them to rendezvous at Lovers

Dream for coffee and for some serious planning.

Alex hurried off to his room. When he got there, he immediately called Milton at the office. "You wouldn't believe it if I told you. I found out some fabulous information last night. I know where the drugs are that Franko plans to smuggle out of here. I also know how he plans to do it. I am to meet Karen for breakfast in a few. Let's plan to meet at noon at Geno's bar. I will fill you in then. In the meantime, I want for you to secretly secure all of the building and underground plans, new and old, for the compound of George de

Garos in the 9th ward. Bring them with you to our meeting."

Milt was so excited about this new information that he almost peed on himself. He was new with the FBI and if he and Alex could solve this case it would mean a great deal for his possibilities for advancement with the agency. Milton called the office to request the information that was requested and then he scrambled to get ready for his lunch meeting with officer Alex. FBI agent Alexander had really taken a liking to Milt and Milton didn't want to do anything to change that. He got dressed and went to the FBI office to get all the information that was requested about George's home and compound. Milt knew that George wasn't foolish enough to store any drugs in his house, but on his property, that was a different matter.

At breakfast Alex and Karen met and discussed the details from the night before. They had really developed a true attraction for each other. The FBI agent knew that this was all wrong, however he also knew that he was to do whatever was needed to secure the information about the illegal transactions which were about to occur. He just didn't know that he was going to fall for this beauty, and she for him. They were like two lovebirds when they met for breakfast.

"We must be careful," said Karen, "because some of my ex-boyfriend's strongmen may be keeping an eye on me. I haven't noticed anyone, but one never knows."

Karen turned to Alex and softly whispered in his ear, "Do you think that after all of this is over, we could run away from it all? We would need to go somewhere where we could not be found. You would have to sell your restaurant in New Mexico, and we could live off of the money and jewels that I have stored up. I will pay Franko off, to keep him off our backs, with some diamonds and he will be satisfied. He doesn't really care for me. He just wants to protect his position with the mob. If I pay him off, he will get his hounds off my trail."

Alex turned red, took a big swallow, and then turned back to his lady and said, "I really think that I am in love with you, and I would like to follow your dreams and plans. For that reason, I must tell you something that might cause you to change your mind about me. This evening let's meet again for dinner, after which we will go to your room, and I will tell you all you need to know about me. I am waiting for a very important call from my associate. After I receive his information, I will feel more at ease to discuss your and my plans of being together."

After breakfast they went their separate ways. Rocky returned with the taxi to take Karen to George's place and Alex took a taxi off to meet Milt at Geno's. There was a great deal that needed to be figured out before dinner, and the lovers' discussion for their immediate future plans. Alex had the cab driver drive around the city while he gathered his thoughts. This would be a major decision. Should the agent give up his position with the FBI and run away with a beautiful lover? He knew that he had to either follow his brain or follow his heart. Love is a strange mental attraction with a very strong influence. He had worked hard to secure the position that he currently held with the FBI and now he was considering giving it all up and running away with the beautiful dream of his life. Maybe a couple of drinks at Geno's bar would make him think more clearly. A talk with Milton would also be beneficial.

"Driver, take me to Geno's bar. I think I can think better there," he blurted out to the cab driver.

As he entered the darkness of Geno's bar, he went to his favorite seat. He messaged Milt and told him that he was there at the bar. Then he ordered a drink, "Give me a double Crown and water, in a small glass and on the rocks. If I fall off of this stool, just prop me up against the wall and wait for my return."

Alex knew the bartender and was always joking with him. The bartender knew when to cut him off and he knew how to get him back to his hotel.

After about 45 minutes, Milt arrived. "I have some more interesting news to show you. Let's go have a seat at a table where I can spread out some of the engineering plans for George's facility."

They went to a table that was rather secluded and Milton spread out the blueprints and began to tell Alex of his findings. "We found that only a small portion of the apartments that George rents out have a living space. They're big enough for a 3-bedroom apartment but they have been built so that the renters will only have a small, 1 bedroom space, like an efficiency. He keeps up the rentals so that the law would think that he has a legitimate business. He obviously stores the drugs in the empty spaces. We also found that George dug a large pit under the area of the present tennis court. He ran all the plumbing around this pit and then he lined it with concrete and sealed it up. The access to the secret storage place is under the toilet of a small adjacent building, which is never rented out. He uses it for his own office."

Alex had heard all he needed to hear. "I will find out if the spaces are full of drugs and when they plan to ship them out," he said. I will get with you in the morning about the details of how we plan to move forward."

Alex had one more double drink with his meal. He and Milt ate a gourmet hamburger topped with a spicy Cajun sauce as they talked about trivia.

Milton said, "You look like you are deep in thought about something. Is there anything on your mind that you want to share with me?"

"Not really, answered Alex. "I am just contemplating a large life change, but I have to make the choice for myself. There is a serious possibility that my job will soon be open. I am going to suggest that you take my place. Please don't share this information with anyone. I want to completely make up my mind before I jump to any decision."

Milt was very shocked by this information, but he was also extremely pleased that he may have an advancement with the FBI coming up soon.

The two men finished their meeting and meal and then parted ways. Alex went back to his room to get a nap and let his Crown Royals wear off. He had a big dinner and evening coming up and he wanted to have his head completely clear.

That evening, about 6:30, Alex met Karen at Lovers Dream restaurant for a quiet lovers' meal. Everything went smoothly and they both were in a great mood.

"Have you thought anymore about the proposition that I whispered in your ear?" asked Karen. "My heart keeps racing just thinking about us being together."

Alex told her that he had been thinking about her, and the proposition, all day. He said that now he wanted to enjoy a fine meal and then retire to her room to discuss future arrangements.

Chapter 4

After their intimate meal, the two lovers headed off to Karen's room. They were no sooner in the room than Alex was lovingly attacked and smothered with kisses. Karen jumped up and wrapped her legs around Alex's waist.

"I have been thinking about this all day. You do not know how hot, just thinking of you, makes me," she said. "I'm going into the other room to change. I have a gown that is much sexier than the one I wore last night."

As Karen left the room, Alex took off his coat and began to get comfortable. He poured two rather stiff Crown Royals and waited for Karen's return.

When she came back in, sure enough she had not been lying. Her new gown was made of black lace which flowed over one shoulder and tucked under the other. There was an elastic band around the waist, which made her entire hourglass shape stand out. There were short pants for her bottoms. These pants were flared at the bottom just over her thighs and there was nothing on underneath. Alex's heart began pounding just looking at her. He handed her the drink that he had made for her, and they both settled down on the couch.

"In order for us to both be lovers and friends, we must hold nothing back from one another," stated Alex.

"I agree completely, and I am prepared to spill my secrets out to you, if you will do the same for me," Karen whispered sexily. "Let me begin first.

"I have already told you that I used to enjoy the company of other men. That was because Franko, my ex-boyfriend, cared nothing about pleasing me. He only cared about pleasing himself. Now that I have found you, I think that I can be totally satisfied. It seems so foolish to rush into a commitment with someone that you barely know but I know what my heart tells me.

"I am only 28 years old, but I have always been tied up with a life of crime and criminal activities. When Franko's men, Franko is my ex-boyfriend, would knock off local jewelry stores, I would go with them just to fill my purse with diamonds and other jewelry. Franko was not interested in the jewelry, only the cash. He thought that jewelry was just a clumsy item that would have to be fenced to get any money out of it. On several occasions Franko and his thugs would get busted for the burglary, but no one ever connected me to any of the jobs. I took the jewels and hid them away from Franko and all the other mobsters. None of them seemed to care. They were too busy with drugs, alcohol, or cold hard cash to be interested in me. I presently have about 10 million dollars' worth of diamond stored away. I can liquidate them, but I have been waiting for the ideal time and place. When I met you, I knew that this is the time, and we could find the place."

Alex just set back with eyes and mouth wide open. He could hardly believe what he was hearing. He knew that all of these details were correct, but he never expected to hear it from Karen, herself.

"Now it is my time to come clean with you," Alex began. "Just promise me that you will not be super mad at me and that you will not throw something at me. After hearing your disclosure, I feel more comfortable about telling you mine."

Karen again settled back into his arms. "You are not really mad with me, are you?" she queried. "I have not been a really good girl. Don't be too angry."

"Just wait until you hear my story," Alex said as he started with his confession. "Please wait until I am completely finished before you question me or decide to walk out on me. I am an active FBI agent in the New Orleans district. I have been sent here to uncover Franko's plans to smuggle drugs into or out of the city. I found that you were working directly with George but then you told me all about him and his operation. My associates got the engineering description for George's complex. We found that they were exactly as you had described. My heart doesn't know exactly what to do. I've fallen in love with you, and I'm prepared to put my entire career behind me, just to be with you. I don't care anything about your jewels or where you have hidden them. I do know that we would need some capital to keep ourselves alive.

"I have already broken so many of the FBI rules," continued Alex, "that I would be thrown off the force anyway. Who cares? It was worth it just being with you. I will certainly not expose any of your illegal dealings, nor will I implicate you in any of the drug smuggling activities. I will tell my associates that you were working for me as an undercover spy and informant.

"If you don't mind me mentioning it, I have an excellent idea," Alex told Karen.

"Go on," she said.

"If I could go with you to the ship that George will use, we could place all the blame on him. The FBI could be called in to make the bust and the only one who will be involved is George and his cronies. Franko can't be angry with you because it was George who screwed up. I'm sure that the diamonds that you plan to use to pay Franko off to leave you alone will go a long way in Franko's paying off the mob for having lost the drug shipment. We will be free and clear to be together and no one will be the wiser."

"You really are a smart FBI agent," whispered Karen. "When do we get started?"

"Wait just a minute," Alex exclaimed. "Are you sure that you are not mad at me for not being a restauranter from New Mexico? Do you still want to go with our plans to be together? I love you so much and I can hardly wait to be totally in your arms."

"What are you waiting for," Karen sighed. "We are just wasting precious time sexy, climb in."

Alex was not far behind.

The following morning, Alex contacted Milton and went over their plans. Alex was to go with Karen to the vessel that George was going to use for smuggling. Together they would make final plans with the captain. George would then come to the ship and make the payment for the work to be done. That was all to be done within one day. The following day, when Alex had given the signal, the FBI would close in on George and his illegal stash of drugs, which were being stored at his 9th ward complex. George would be arrested, and all of the drugs would be seized. George's compound would be rearranged so as not to be accessible to storing any illegal matter of any kind. No more illegal drugs. No more illegal human trafficking. Basically, no more George.

All Alex's plans were followed to the letter. All the local people who were involved with the crimes were rounded up and prosecuted. George was sent away for a very long time and Franko was not aware of any of these actions. Karen paid Franko off in diamonds just to leave her alone and let her have her private life. Alex retained his position with the FBI but he was given a raise and a promotion. Milton jumped into Alex's old position. Alex and Karen bought a small, but nice, house where they set up housekeeping. Was this one of those stories where only the good guys win? Well, I guess if you call Alex and Karen good guys, yes it was.

Story # 2: The Fishermen

Chapter 1

He was a crotchety old man, and as ornery as one comes. If you didn't have something in common to discuss with him, you had best just steer clear. If one got to know him well, he could be a rather likable friend, but not too friendly because he always maintained that strictness, pomp and circumstances with which he had lived for 43 years of strict military service.

Tim was in the United States Air Force for a good part of his life. They were mostly good years which allowed him to marry and raise a family. They were also trying years which put sternness and discipline in the forefront of most everything that he did.

He was, as most military people are, transferred to many various assignment locations. Sometimes he was allowed to take his family but sometimes he was sent alone. Most of the alone assignments were when he was sent into a battle or combat zone. He spent several years in Korea and several in Vietnam, where he served as a surgeon with the medical division of the Air Force.

No one can really know the feeling of sewing up wounded soldiers just to send them back, after they healed, into combat. No one can really know the feeling of trying your best to save the life of a wounded soldier, only to see it slip away on the operating table. It's difficult to know the difficulty of performing surgery in second rate conditions, only to lose power and not be able to complete the surgical task. None of this can really be known unless you have lived it for yourself. It is very easy to see how men of combat, or of medicine, could be hardened to many aspects of life.

On one occasion, Dr. Tim was in the process of surgically removing two bullets from a young soldier's chest. Mortar fire began coming into the entire mobile medical camp. One round hit immediately outside of his surgery suite. The explosion caused the generators to be yielded nonfunctional and thus the entire operating suite lost all lighting and electricity.

Tim, being the commanding officer of the surgical unit, began barking out orders, which had to be quickly and immediately addressed. The nurses and the operating surgeons moved the patients that were presently undergoing surgery outside of the tent facility. When outside, they were blessed with the dim light of the full moon. The available nurses grabbed flashlights and the surgeons completed their tasks. Sternness and discipline were of the utmost importance at this time. It was a terrible situation, but it was the one that they had been given.

When the shelling and surgery was over, the entire medical staff retired to their own living quarters, which were located in an adjacent tent. An eerie calm and quietness engulfed the entire tent as a bottle of vodka was quietly opened and passed around. Some of the nurses were so frightened from the recent events, especially the explosions, that they sought comfort in the doctors' tent. As usual, they were welcomed with open arms.

On another occasion, Dr. Tim and his fellow surgeons were greeted with nine wounded soldiers at one time. The ambulance had delivered the wounded soldiers, but no one had yet triaged them. Since they didn't know who was injured the worst and needed immediate attention, Tim jumped into the arriving ambulances and began barking out orders as to who should be taken to surgery first. Everyone listened to, and obeyed, his every command. They knew of his competence and skill as a medical practitioner and knew that his orders were correct and should be strictly followed. Again, that was the building of a stern and well-disciplined man. Not just a man, but a man of honor.

There were many occasions in which the strict orders and commands of this hardened surgeon had to be followed to the letter.

Tim was rather lucky because he served his later years as a surgeon in a fine military hospital in the States. He retired as a full colonel at a fairly early age and then was allowed to pursue his true ambitions of fishing and boating. Luckily for Tim, his last assignment with the military was close to the water where he could pursue his hobbies. There were also many military personnel living in this location, with which he could befriend and enjoy many of his hobbies and activities.

There were several close fishing buddies with whom he enjoyed sharing his time on the water. One in particular was Harry. Tim and Harry experimented with all sorts of boating endeavors.

Early one morning, before the first light, these two fishermen decided to run out to the barrier islands to do some fishing. They had heard that the bull reds were running around the bars of the islands. Harry had an 18-foot boat with a 125hp outboard motor. Both fishermen, not having a great deal of experience on Gulf waters, thought that this boat was certainly large enough to take whatever the massive body of water had to dish out. They were terribly wrong.

As the would-be explorers traveled due south the waves became larger and larger. It was still dark so they could not see how large the waves actually were. Finally, after both men had enough of being beaten around by the sea, Tim became rather hostile.

"Give me the damn spotlight", Tim ordered. Harry plugged it in and handed it to Tim, who immediately turned it on and shone the light toward the bow. At that same time a large wave came crashing completely over the entire boat.

"What the hell", Harry screamed out.

"Where did that big wave come from?" Tim pointed the light again to the bow where a second large wave was coming over the bow rail and into the small boat.

"They're everywhere," Tim exclaimed. "Turn this &*^%#** boat around before we are completely swamped."

Both of the fishermen were rushing to get their life jackets on. Their hearts were beating so fast that it was difficult to get the jacket's buckles connected. Harry immediately swung the boat around from due south to due north. He hit the throttle which caused the boat to plunge forward. By this forward motion, a lot of the water that they had taken on washed out the stern. One of the tackle boxes washed out along with the excess water.

"Do you think we should go back and get it? Inquired Harry.

"Hell no," said Tim. "It's not even light yet and we couldn't see the box, besides, it was one of your tackle boxes. I'm not about to head back into those nasty seas."

The entire way back home the two grumbled about not being able to fish. They were still trembling from the scare and neither wanted to attempt the journey again. When they got back to the mainland, they stopped at a pay phone and called one of their wives. They reported that they were back in, and they were going to do a little inshore fishing before coming home.

The sea breeze was blowing about 20 knots. Most of the local waters were stirred up and had little visibility. The entire day of fishing was a bummer. All wasn't lost, however. Tim had the bright idea of them stopping at a liquor store and picking up some gin and tonic. This sounded like a good idea to Harry so away they went.

When they returned to the boat, they found that they had tied it too tightly and it couldn't compensate for the rapidly incoming tide. The boat was almost swamped again.

They got into the boat and headed off to calmer waters. Immediately they both poured themselves a stiff gin and tonic. One drink led to another. Before long, neither of the men could see, let alone drive the boat.

Since Harry lived on a bayou, they decided to beach the boat and walk back to his house. When arriving at the house, Harry's wife met them at the front door.

"What are y'all doing coming in the front? The boat dock is in the back."

"Well, it's like this," Harry began. "We drank too much, and we lost the boat."

"What about your tackle?" inquired Harry's wife.

Tim spoke up, "We lost the whole damn thing."

The next morning the two fishermen headed down the bayou where they found the boat beached near some tall pines.

"What a hell of a day," Harry said.

The next morning, he listed the boat for sale. He said that if he ever takes Tim out fishing again, they will have a bigger boat.

Chapter 2

The next time Harry and Tim went fishing together, a year or so had passed. Both men had gained a little more knowledge and skill at boating and fishing. Harry and Tim both had their own boats now and often they would compete with each other as to who would catch the most fish.

When the Ling began to bite in their area, the two would usually go together and fish from one of their boats. Harry decided, what the hell, Tim could not be any more demanding than he was on the day the boat almost sank from swamping. At least they had learned enough not to lose the boat anymore.

All the proper tackle was loaded into the boat. They had gotten special bait and chum for fishing for the ling. About 30 miles offshore, they encountered several of the local shrimping boats that had anchored up for the day. The shrimpers usually shrimp at night. They throw overboard their bycatch during the early morning, which usually attracts many types of fish, especially the ling.

Harry pulled his boat close to the stern of the large shrimper. The fishermen were still up cleaning their nets.

"Do you mind if we tie up behind you? We're trying to catch some ling. We would be happy to give you a 6 pack of cold beer," said Tim.

That was all it took. Within 10 minutes the two friends were tied up behind the shrimp boat. Instantly they could see the silvery sides of several fish plunging through the water and eating the scraps from the shrimper. Within fifteen minutes, Tim spotted two sizable ling swimming toward the boat. He called out to Harry and told him to be prepared for some good fighting and then good eating.

Tim hooked a nice ling and fought it for about 20 minutes. When he brought it close to the boat, Harry got excited and grabbed the gaff. He gaffed the fish, who was still not tired out. His arm jerked and the fish rapidly swam off with the tackle broken and no fish in sight. Tim screamed a few foul words at Harry and then they began to fish for another ling.

After about an hour, Tim hooked up with another ling. This one was bigger than the first. Jim had to fight it for almost 40 minutes before he brought it to the side of the boat.

"Don't try to gaff him until I give the command," Tim ordered.

Harry was already upset for having lost Jim's first fish. He held the gaff up out of the water so as not to disturb Tim's fight with the fish. Soon the fish was tired out and Tim brought it up along the side.

"Okay. Now it is okay for you to gaff him, just be careful," said Tim.

Harry leaned over the side of the boat and aimed the gaff directly toward the large fish. The fish whirled around and hit the hook and leader line directly onto the gaff. The hook pulled out and the fish was gone in a flash. All the blood rushed out of the face of Harry when he faced Tim for his scolding.

"You stupid, lamebrained, idiotic, clumsy, worthless piece of &*^%. I have caught two ling and you have released them both," hollered Tim. "Remind me to get another fishing partner for my next trip."

The orders and cursing came flying out of Tim's mouth faster than the bullets out of a machine gun.

"Where did you learn those expletives?" asked Harry. "Certainly not from the military."

Two hours had passed, and the men were about to cast away from their shrimper. The men on the shrimp boat were asleep so they tried to be as quiet as possible. Harry reached over to the large, empty ice chest on the starboard side of the boat. He opened the chest and just stood there staring at the ice. Just as he released the tie line from the large boat, Tim called out that he had hooked another ling.

"You stay away," Tim yelled. "I'll get him in by myself".

As the third ling was brought within gaffing distance, Harry reached for the gaff.

"Hold on," cried Tim. "This is your final chance. If you miss this one, there is no more fishing with me."

Harry stood at the ready, his jaw fixed and his muscles bulging.

"You just bring him here," Harry said. "I'll show you what fishing is all about. The fish was guided into position by Tim. Harry grabbed the gaff and made one swift swing at the fish. The gaff sunk deep into the flesh of the fish. Harry used all his strength to swing the fish out of the water, over both of their heads and directly into the open ice chest.

"Damn," said Tim. "That fish must have been fifty pounds. How did you do that?"

Harry just giggled and said under his breath, "That's the way I always do it. I was just practicing the first two times."

Six months later Harry got a call from Tim, "You gotta see my new fishing boat. I saw it advertised and I just had to have it. We no longer have to worry about how bad the seas are or how far we can go out. We just get in this baby and go fishing."

Harry knew that something was up when Tim said that he wanted Harry to go on the boat's "maiden voyage".

"Where do you plan to go fishing," Harry inquired.

"This baby has twin diesel engines and will go about 35 mph. It only uses a small amount of fuel because it's diesel. This boat doesn't use but 5 gallons an hour, cruising at 28mph.

We can run down to the oil rigs within about 3 hours, and we will only use about 15 gallons of fuel. The boat has two fuel tanks and holds a total of 60 gallons," Tim bragged. "At 15 gallons of fuel used for our trip down and 15 gallons for our return, we will have 30 gallons of fuel to use running around the oil rigs and fishing."

The two fishermen, explorers, loaded the 32-foot boat with enough food to last for weeks and enough beer and water to last longer than that. They didn't intend staying out that long, but they planned on drinking up all of the beer before they returned.

"How long do we plan to stay out on this trip?" Harry asked excitedly.

"Oh hell, we will probably be back within 2 or 3 days," was Tim's reply. "If we are catching fish, who cares how long we stay out?"

At 6 a.m. the duo of makeshift fishermen headed due south on Tim's new launch. When they reached the barrier islands, Tim steered the boat on course to go directly to the desired oil rigs. Tim then took Harry to the engine room where they inspected the two diesels.

"They are humming like kittens" Tim announced. "Do you see this small fuel valve? It goes directly to the two fuel tanks. We have been running on the starboard tank since we left port but I am going to change it so we will run on both tanks and use an equal amount of fuel from each. When we get there, we can turn it back to one single tank. This way we will always know how much fuel we have on board," Tim called out with complete confidence, and clarity of knowledge, of his new boat.

The sportsmen, along with their trusted vessel traveled along smoothly. They kept it at about 22 knots to conserve the fuel. Within about 3 hours of cruising, they could see the first oil rig that they wanted to fish.

"There she blows," exclaimed Tim, who was at the helm. He kicked the engines up to a cruising speed of 28 mph. After about 30 minutes, at the increased speed, both engines began to sputter. One completely shut down and the other ran at a much slower speed.

"What the hell?" What is going on here?" asked Tim.

Harry jumped down into the engine room and began searching for the problem.

"It sounds to me like the engines are not getting fuel," said Harry. "I know you said that we would have plenty enough, but would you mind checking the fuel gauges again."

When Tim looked at the gauges, he found that they were completely out of fuel.

"How could this be?" Tim cried out. "I had calculated all of the fuel consumptions correctly and now we are completely out of fuel."

Harry looked directly at the small fuel valve that Tim had opened to allow fuel to flow from each engine.

"Look directly behind us and see what you see," hollered Harry. "I'll bet you see a long stream of diesel fuel trailing us. When you turned the fuel valve, you mistakenly turned to the position that says 'discard.' All of the way out here the fuel has been being discarded overboard. We were running on both tanks but at the same time, the fuel contents were being pumped overboard.

"Damn it, damn it, damn it. I think that you are just a curse for my fishing," yelled Tim.

Harry said, "Well at least we always have a great story to tell. What are we going to do now?"

Harry noticed that they had traveled directly into the active oil fields, off Louisiana.

"Let's have another cold beer and wait until a crew boat comes along. They will be servicing the wells, and we may be able to buy some diesel fuel from one of them."

"It's a damn good thing that these engines are diesel. No other boat out here uses gasoline," Tim exclaimed.

The two sat in their motionless launch for about an hour waiting for a diesel crew boat to come along. As soon as they saw one, they hailed him down on the VHF radio and he came directly to them.

"What's the problem," called the captain.

Harry called back, "This blockhead turned the wrong fuel cock and we dumped all of our fuel overboard. Is it possible for us to buy some diesel fuel from you?"

"Certainly," the captain replied. I carry 800 gallons in my auxiliary tank and 5000 gallons in my main tank. I will pump you some out of my auxiliary tank. How much do you need?"

Tim told the congenial captain that they only needed 60 gallons to top it off.

After the boat received the fuel from the crew boat, Tim asked him how much he owed him.

"Oh hell no," was his reply. "I dump more fuel overboard than that just trying to fill one of the generators on an oil rig. The boss won't even know it's gone."

The crew boat captain was not in a big hurry to get to his next assignment. Tim and Harry tied their boat to the larger boat and climbed aboard.

"Where are y'all headed from here?" the captain queried.

Tim spoke up immediately, "We 're headed straight back in to port. I am so afraid of having Harry on my boat that I want to get in before something else happens."

They all sat down and had a big picnic lunch, complete with adequate cold beer.

After several more trips fishing for larger fish, Tim and Harry decided that they would focus on catching trout and redfish. Fishing in the Louisiana marshes was their favorite spot. Tim got more into the trout fishing than did Harry.

Tim became very proficient at that type of sport. It was almost never that he would come in from a fishing trip with less than his limit of tasty fresh fish. Although it cost a lot to hire a guide, it was less expensive than buying your own boat and paying for fuel, upkeep, bait, and insurance.

Both Tim and Harry had become more mellow in their old age, especially about fishing. They still enjoyed the challenge of fishing but let someone else do the boat upkeep and the cleaning of the fish. They were perfectly happy to take home cleaned fish that were ready to cook.

Speaking of cooking, Tim turned out to be an expert on cooking fish in many ways. They were all very delicious and Tim was always prepared to share. Now the fishing trips were much more enjoyable and laidback. Fresh fish caught from someone else's boat, with someone else's bait and tackle, with someone else cleaning the catch and the boat, what could be better than that?

STORY #3: Black Bart, the Pirate

CHAPTER 1

As the sun was setting behind them and the full moon was just breaking the horizon off the bow, the captain gave the order to "Hoist the main, fore and aft, and let this fair breeze give fulness to the two main jibs. Step lively mates and ye shall soon see the glitter of gold so generously given by the King of Portugal, the Queen of Spain, and the King of England."

He hardly ever called out the commands to the entire crew. That was the job of the first mate, however this was going to be a memorable voyage for the entire ship's family. They were all as one and they cared sincerely for their fellow sailors. There was no hesitation when the captain called out the orders, for they all knew that they were under the command of one of the finest captains that sailed the high seas.

This was the ship of Captain Bartholomew Roberts, better known as "Black Bart," the most successful pirate from England to Spain and across the Atlantic to North America. His realm spread from Barbados in the south to Africa on the east and from the rich Gulf of Mexico on the west, up the east coast of North America and across the vast Atlantic to the Mediterranean and Italy.

On this fine sailing night, Bart and his crew were sailing out of Jamaica and headed to Cuba for some extra rum and other rations. After their brief stopover in Havana, they were sailing north to Nassau in the Bahamas. There Captain Roberts would recruit some worthy fighting men to accompany him eastward to Africa.

They were not so interested in what Africa had to offer them. What they really desired was to encounter some of the trade ships from Europe. They had all intentions of lightening the trade ships of their load of gold and silver. Bart knew that the trade ships would be laden with precious metals and would be headed to Africa to buy some slaves and transport them across the Sargassum Sea, where they would sell them and trade them for precious sugar, which was plentiful in the Caribbean Islands and throughout the Antilles.

Captain Roberts' pirate ship, no matter which one he was sailing at the time, was named "FORTUNE." On it he always found fortune, not despair. A pirate's ship was as much a part of his family as any of his crew. It was respected and defended at all costs. Every pirate knew that his first allegiance was to his captain. After the captain, the pirates' allegiance was to his ship. Without the ship, there would be no pirate, no precious bounty, and no future of debauchery on the seas.

Roberts, his crew and ship, along with all other pirates who sailed the main, had a gut-wrenching hatred for any ship that was traveling with slaves. It mattered not where the ships were from nor where they were destined, the trade ship would immediately be boarded, the slaves freed, and the ship and its crew would be burned. Often the crew of such a trade ship would be spared from burning by being hanged from the yardarm before the ship was torched.

It was an interesting sight to see the swift sailing pirate vessels approaching the trade ships and boarding them like they were simply boards with paddles. It was rather curious why the trade ships, when seeing the pirate ships approaching, would lower their sails and surrender to the invaders. The pirates never showed mercy on the traders and only kept them alive long enough to locate all their gold.

Each ship from the various countries would fly its own colors. It was easy for all at sea to determine where the ship was from simply by seeing the national flag that it was flying. The pirates, however, were harder to identify. Some of them had all black colors. Many of them put a symbol of bones of humans on their colors. It became a custom for many pirates to place a skull and cross bones on their flags. Still, one must get close enough to determine if the bones were red or white.

Captain Roberts had such hatred for many of the islanders from many of the islands that he put cross bones in the middle of his flag with characters of the different islands in the four corners. No matter which pirate was looting a trade ship, it was always too late for the traders to properly respond and take evasive actions.

Luckily for many slaves, they were usually offered a place on the ship with the pirates. If they chose not to be a pirate, they would be released on the nearest island upon which the pirates landed. Many of the black Africans that worked the sugar fields and plantations of the islands were not sold to their owners by slave traders but left unattended on an island by some group of pirates. Either way, they were just slaves to the workings of the various plantations.

It was unimaginable for one to visualize the lives that were led by these plantation slaves. They had little or no food, medications, shelter, or clothing. They worked in the scorching Caribbean sun for almost all of every day. Although many of the plantation owners did not heed the law, the slaves were not supposed to be required to work on Sundays. On some few occasions, slaves were able to make enough money by working off the plantation on Sundays to purchase their freedom. They could then buy land and have their own slaves. The circle of man's inhumanity to his fellow man just kept running its course.

CHAPTER 2

After Captain Roberts had gathered the adequate number of pirates for him to continue his voyage, he made it known that he had completed his registration. There were many pirates hanging around the port of Nassau who wanted to be a part of Bart's crew. Although there were many cutthroats and thieves on the docks, there was a limited number of quality shipmen and sailors. These men not only had to know how to fight, but they also had to know all there was to know about tending a sailing vessel. They needed to know how to properly care for the sails and the massive rigging. They had to know how to dress the course of their ship so that it would overtake trade ships. Speed and safety were the keywords for the pirate sailors.

Each pirate, as he boarded the ship, was assigned a bunk. This bunk was made up of a simple swinging hammock made of durable canvas. The bunks hung side by side of other pirates in their sleeping quarters. It was seen that each sailor had either a gold ring in their ear or on their hand. These gold rings were provided so that the shipmate of each pirate could remove it, upon the other pirate's death, and use it to pay for a decent burial. Most of the time the burials were at sea, in which case the man was wrapped in his canvas hammock, accompanied by a stone to weigh the body down, and thrown overboard. There was little pomp and circumstance connected to these burials.

The rules for being a pirate were very strict, however, their bondage to one another was very strong. On every sailing ship, the captain and his officers were held in highest regard. It was a capital offense for a pirate crewman to disobey the orders of an officer. He was subjected to several choices of punishment. The offending crewman could be hung from the rigging of the ship. He could be caused to walk the plank, or just be thrown overboard which was easier but it didn't give the enjoyment to the on-watching pirates. Another punishment given out to disobedient sailors was to be keelhauled. This means exactly what it says. A line is run under the hull of the boat and over the keel. It was then affixed to both sides of the ship. A sailor was tied to one side of the ship and dragged under the hull to the other side of the ship. The barnacles on the underside of the ship were not conducive to a smooth trip under the boat. The sailor was severely scratched and torn. If the sailor were to live to reach the other side of the ship, without being eaten by sharks or bleeding to death, he would be considered having served his punishment sentence. If the sailor were to survive from the possible infections which would develop in his wounds from his severe scratching by barnacles, he would then be reinstated as a full mate with his crew.

Often pirates, or officers, would be seen wearing an eyepatch over one eye. This was not because they had lost one eye, although it looked good in battle. The reason for the eye patch was so that one eye would be accustomed to light and the other to dark. Below deck, on one of these vessels, it was extremely dark. Often the officers, or a crewman, was required to go below. When this was required, the sailor simply switched the patch from one eye to the other, allowing him to see immediately. There were no windows, just the ports through which the cannons were protruded. These cannon holes were opened only when they were in a skirmish with another ship.

Other than at these times, there was little to no light below deck. There were one or two small candles which were protected by glass encasements; however, they were small and put off very little light. These candles were carefully watched and monitored. A fire below deck could cost many lives and even perhaps the life of the ship itself.

In the bowels of the vessel were kept several buckets which were used to collect excrement. Besides the terrible odor produced by the waste product, it also produced methane gas. It didn't take the officers long to figure out what made their candle lights explode if the methane was allowed to build up. It was a serious offense for a crew member not to empty his crapper after each use. No one wanted for an unexplained fire to break out below deck.

Above deck there were always chores to be done. The pirates would be responsible for swabbing the deck every day. All the rigging and supplies were cleaned and kept in first class condition. Often the sails were unfurled, simply to check them out properly and see that they were ready to enter into battle.

Since there were no dining facilities, all possible room was taken for cannons, powder and supplies, meals were eaten on deck. There were very few scraps left over from a meal but that which did remain were thrown overboard to feed the sharks that were always trailing the ship looking for a free handout. A pirate ship was a serious, well-planned machine which was treated that way and manned by expert sailors and pirates.

CHAPTER 3

Fortune was sailed out of the harbor of Nassau, around the neighboring small islands, and out to sea. Everyone knew that it would be several months before they saw, or touched, dry land again. Those wives and girlfriends left behind were the least of the pirates' worries. They were now at sea and each of them had to think about saving his own life, and the life of the ship.

During their spare time, the pirates would sharpen their sabers and see to the maintenance of the cannons and handguns. Powder was kept dry by storing it in large barrels, next to the cannons below deck. Above deck there were only small splatter cannons, which were mounted on the railings. These splatter guns were filled with all sorts of small metal objects. They were shot at the deck of the ship which they were capturing. This splattering effect was usually enough to completely clear the deck's sailors from the other ship. The splatter guns were capable of being moved to whichever side of the pirate ship was closest to the ship being invaded. There were mounts on the railing of either side which were made to accept and hold the splatter cannons firmly in place. One pirate was assigned to each of the two splatter guns. He would man the cannon until they came alongside the invaded ship, at which time he would join the other pirates in boarding the other ship and taking command.

Two days after Fortune had sailed into the open Atlantic, they encountered their first trade ship. It was heavily laden with precious metals and jewels to trade with the Caribbean plantation owners for the precious sugar that Europeans desperately desired. This trade ship flew the colors of Spain and was headed directly to the Caribbean. There were no slaves on board since this ship was being used for sugar trade only. The name of this ship was the Tia Maria and it carried only 4 cannons for defense.

Black Bart recognized this ship as being one that he had sailed on as a child. He had learned much about sailing aboard this grand ship. Nevertheless, he planned to relieve it of its precious gold cargo. Immediately, Captain Roberts hoisted his colors of a black flag with crossed human bones and the four symbols in each corner. This informed the trade ship that the Fortune was a pirate ship.

As Captain Bart made his vessel ready for battle, he took his place on the foredeck railing with a cup of English tea. Never would the captain consume rum, or any alcoholic beverage, before he entered battle. From his drinking of tea, he gained the name of "Teetotaler," which was what he was known by many of the professional sailors.

The Tia Maria hoisted all its available sails and tried to outrun the oncoming pirates. This was a futile effort for the Fortune was a much faster ship. Soon it was alongside the trader. The first mate of the Fortune used a bull horn to instruct the other ship to lower its sails. They fired one blast of their cannons across the bow of the Tia Maria. The captain of the trade ship quickly realized that he was out gunned by a very fast pirate ship. His sails were stricken, and the ship came about and readied itself to be boarded.

As the Fortune laid itself alongside the Tia Maria, the pirates immediately boarded the trade ship. They had their sabers drawn and their pistols in hand. The captain and crew of the Tia Maria were on deck and none of them were armed. At first the pirates didn't know what to think. Captain Roberts then boarded the captured ship and directly walked over to the captain.

"Good day captain John Smith. Are you keeping well?" said Black Bart.

Captain Smith replied that he was doing well, and he inquired about the wellbeing of Captain Roberts. Both men shook hands, and they began a lengthy conversation. Both ships simply drifted at sea as they were bound together by strong boarding lines.

When the conversation was over, Captain Roberts informed Captain Smith that he was obliged to remove half of his gold bounty and all of the precious jewels that were on board. He left Captain Smith with the other half of the gold so that he might continue on to do his trading for sugar.

Captain Bart said, "Either peacefully render over half of your gold and all of your jewels or I will have my crew remove all of your gold and jewels, hang you from the yardarm and set fire to your ship. I realize that we were sailing mates back in the day, but we must now do what we must do."

Captain Smith readily handed over the bounty that was requested. He thanked Captain Bart for not taking all his trading gold and he bid him farewell.

The pirates were directed to reboard their own ship and make ready to sail. They all considered the act of not taking but half of the bounty from the trader, but they reasoned that the half gold and jewels from the trader, without a fight, was better than fighting and possibly losing some strategic men. The pirates would all get their cut of the captured goods. Although it was less than what they could have had, it was much better than fighting for it.

The Fortune was untied from the trader, and it hoisted its main sail. As it calmly drifted away from the Tia Maria, Black Bart retook his position of drinking his tea from the bow railing. He considered this to be a good and successful day. Gold and jewels were gained, and no one was injured or died. Besides that, his tea was brewed just right for his liking.

CHAPTER 4

Sailing for the Fortune was very calm and peaceful for several days. There were no storms in the Atlantic and the weather looked fair. The men worked diligently readying their ship for a possible future battle. In the evenings there was often the sound of a harmonica and some singing. The captain didn't mind the singing because it was so far off key that it kept the sea monsters away. He really believed that because they were never bothered by giant squids or rogue whales. Other ships reported sightings of many strange and bizarre things, such as mermaids and fire breathing dragons, but Fortune never encountered any of these things. Could it have been the terrible singing? Who knows?

They were headed southeast, directly toward the Sargassum sea, which stretched from the isle of Verde and the Canary Islands in northwest Africa to the windward and leeward islands of the Caribbean to the west. Here they would probably encounter trade ships which were carrying slaves to be traded and sold in the islands to the west. These slave ships would be carrying little gold bounty because they had spent most of it on buying slaves. The only reason to attack any of these ships was the pleasure of freeing the captured slaves. It also gave the pirates a real-life battle session and practice in boarding captive ships. Depending on the mood of Captain Bart, some of the captured ship's officers would be hung or simply thrown overboard. If the slave ships were found to be treating the slaves humanely, they would be spared from burning and being lost at sea. Nothing irritated Captain Roberts more than to find that the captain of a slave trading ship was treating his cargo of African captives inhumanely. Some captains allowed the slaves to walk around the deck for exercise. Others simply packed the slaves below deck and only provided water and a little bread.

About 300 miles WNW (west-north-west), or 280 degrees by the magnetic compass from the center of the Sargassum sea, the Fortune encountered its first trade ship that was loaded with slaves and destined for Jamaica. As the Fortune approached the trader, they noticed that it was flying Portuguese flag colors. This meant that the ship was commanded by stern and combative officers. They would not readily release their cargo, nor would they peacefully allow themselves to be boarded.

The captain of the Fortune delivered his orders and intentions to the first mate, who in turn conveyed them to his acting officers. Their sails were to be rendered full and they were to achieve full speed ahead to intercept the Portuguese ship. As they approached, they could see that the name of the ship was the Bella Luna. It had hoisted all its sails in order to outrun the approaching pirate ship. There was little need for their sails because Fortune was the swiftest sailing vessel on the seas. If they were to be outrun, the escaping ship would need to have a very large head start, which the Bella Luna did not have.

As the Fortune drew close and fired its warning cannon, the Bella Luna furled its main sails and turned so that it would be broadside to the approaching pirates. It was well armed with four cannons on both the port and the starboard sides. All four of the trade ship's port side cannons rang out, sending large metal cannon balls directly toward the Fortune. The balls passed to the bow and the stern of the pirate ship. The only harm that was done was to anger the pirates into a direct attack.

The Fortune steered directly perpendicular to the Bella Luna and speedily made way to within a couple of hundred yards from its mark. It swiftly turned broadside to the trader and unloaded six cannons directly at the ship being attacked. The six cannons were quickly followed by the report of six more cannons from the same side of Fortune. Six of the twelve cannonballs found their mark on the Bella Luna, one striking the fore mast and one striking the main mast. The other four tore large holes in the sails of their main and jibs. Fortune immediately turned directly into the Bella Luna, so as to avoid making a large target at which the trader might shoot.

The pirates approached within 100 yards of the trade ship, at which time they fired their deck mounted scatter cannons. Metal shrapnel pelleted the deck of the Bella Luna and wounded several of their crew. Knowing that they were outgunned and outmaneuvered, the Bella Luna hoisted a large white flag of surrender. Fortune laid against the trade ship's side and the pirates immediately boarded it.

There was little resistance from the Bella Luna, however, a few men refused to lay down their arms and fired their pistols at the pirates. These Portuguese men soon lost their shooting arm and were then thrown overboard by the pirates.

When all was finally calmed on the deck of the captured ship, Captain Roberts officially boarded the Bella Luna to take control. His first move was to go below and see the condition of the slaves. It was horrible. The slaves were packed in small bunks, 3 persons high and 40 persons wide. They were all chained to their bunks where they were unable to move or exercise.

The smell below was unbearable. The feces of the slaves was just allowed to fall to the person below and then down to the floor, where it piled up and was never cleaned out. Urine was also just allowed to fall to the person below. There was a small metal ladle which was used to pass small amounts of water to the slaves, if it was not consumed by another slave before it got passed along. There were barrels of molded bread, in the form of biscuits. These biscuits were passed around as food for the many slaves.

Roberts immediately ordered his men to release all the slaves. Four of the 120 slaves had already died, and their bodies were taken up on deck for a proper funeral. After the dead slaves were committed to the sea, Black Bart proceeded to deal with the officers and crew of the slave ship. There were two slaves that could understand English, which was what Captain Bart spoke. They were directed to ask the slaves if there were any of the slave trading crew that treated them more inhumanely than did others. Six of Bella Luna's crew were pointed out as being excessively cruel to the slaves. These six men were immediately strung up and hung from the yardarms. They were allowed to hang there while Roberts administered justice to the rest of the crew and officers.

There were only four officers, including the captain, and twelve crew members who were sailing the Bella Luna. The officers were asked if there was any gold or valuables on the ship. One of the officers stepped forward and revealed the location of the treasures. Although there was little to choose from, the pirates helped themselves to what there was. The officer that disclosed where the treasure was to be found, was told that he was a traitor to his country. He was then offered a position as a mate on the crew of the Fortune, which he immediately accepted.

Roberts ordered the crew of the slave ship to go below and clean up the filthy mess that was left by the chained slaves. He then gathered the entire remaining crew and the officers of the Bella Luna. He told them that he was going to destroy most of their sails but would leave enough for them to sail to the nearest Island and release all of the slaves. Captain Roberts also had his men go around the trade ship and, in many places, substantially mark by chopping into the wood so that he might recognize the ship should he come upon it again. He told the captain, officers, and crew of the Bella Luna that if he boarded their vessel again and found that it was transporting slaves, he would hang all of the crew, throw the officers overboard and burn the ship.

With this, Roberts and all the pirates returned to the Fortune and merrily sailed away. It would certainly be possible for the freed slaves to rebel against the men of the Bella Luna, however, that was something that they alone would have to deal with.

CHAPTER 5

Captain Roberts plotted a course for his ship that would take them back northward toward the Cape Verde Islands and directly into the path of the trade ships that would be laden with treasures and gold. He was trying to target the ships that had not yet spent their King or Queen's money on the purchase of slaves.

Roberts would have to attack the ships north of Ghana and south of the Canary Islands. This was exactly where these pirates headed. They had high expectations of filling their coffers with loads of silver and gold, along with any precious jewelry that they could find.

The sailing was smooth all the way across the Atlantic. Roberts and his men had plenty of time to get their vessel in shipshape. The cannons were tended, the sabers sharpened, and the rum barrels were safely stored. Everyone was assigned his own limit of grog for daily consumption. The captain wanted all his pirates to stay happy and satisfied but he would not allow any drunkenness on board. There was no telling when they might encounter a trade ship and want to launch an assault.

Sure enough, just as soon as Fortune reached within 100 miles of the Canary Islands, they encountered a large Spanish trader. It appeared that this ship was laden with treasure and headed for Africa to purchase slaves. This was a large ship and would be capable of carrying some 300 slaves, if they were packed into it properly. Just the thought of this possible slave trade turned the stomach of all the pirates and their officers.

Captain Roberts quickly adjusted his course so his ship would intercept the slave trading Spanish vessel. They swiftly sailed to within striking distance of their intended target. The pirates could easily see the Spanish colors that the ship was flying, and they could make out the ship's name. It was the Tia Alicia de Barcelona, and it was well equipped with cannons to fend off any invader.

Fortune maneuvered itself into position to stop the Alicia, either by firing warning shots or by disabling the vessel by using its cannons. A warning shot was fired by the pirates, which barely missed the Spanish ship's bow. The Alicia immediately swung into the wind and unloaded six of its cannons directly at Fortune.

The pirates were surprised because most ships lower their sails and yielded when they were attacked by a pirate ship. This Alicia was spunky and ready for a fight.

"So shall it be," hollowed the pirate crew as they wielded away, made a complete circle and lined themselves up parallel to the Alicia, about 200 yards away.

Bart had the distinct advantage because he had equipped his ship with smaller cannons that could reach longer distances. Six of his cannons rang out sending solid steel balls directly to the Spanish ship's tall masts. With a loud crack, two of the masts of the Alicia were broken off when hit with the long-range balls.

The Alicia's cannons again rang out, sending their cannon balls straight toward the Fortune. All six of the balls fell yards short of their mark. The Spanish vessel had large, powerful cannons that were effective only at short ranges and

Black Bart, sitting on the bow rails and sipping his morning tea, stayed just out of range of the Spanish cannons.

The pirates quickly prepared their cannons and set them aiming directly toward the Alicia. Six of the cannons were directed to the masts of their enemies while six more were aimed at the hull of the Spanish vessel. The first six cannons were fired, followed immediately by six more.

The cannon balls found their targets. One more of the masts of the Alicia was broken off and much of its sails was destroyed. The other six balls found their way to the hull of the Alicia, breaking off much of the railing of the ship and disabling two of her main cannons. One of the balls from the Fortune found its way to the waterline of the Spanish ship, which caused the vessel to begin taking on water.

The Alicia was now disabled from sailing, but she still had protective cannons that could keep Fortune away and at a distance. The pirates realized this and ignored firing their cannons at Alicia's sails and rigging. They directed all twelve cannons to the hull, and especially the cannons of their adversary. Six cannons again rang out from Fortune, followed in a few seconds by six more.

All twelve of the steel balls found their mark on the hull of the Alicia. Four of them completely disabled Four more of Alicia's cannons. This left them with only one functional cannon with which to defend herself. Still, she would not hoist the white flag of surrender.

Captain Bart directed his ship to speedily approach the wounded Spanish ship from its stern. When they got within range to be very accurate, the pirates fired four cannons directly at the only functional cannon that Alicia had. The cannon was struck by two of the balls and it also was rendered incapable of firing.

The pirate ship then sailed from Alicia's stern to directly alongside the disabled Spanish ship. When they got close to Alicia, the Spanish crew opened fire on Fortune with their muskets and pistols. Fortune returned fire with two of her scatter cannons which wounded most of the crew and cleared the deck.

The pirates threw grappling hooks onto the Alicia and pulled her aside the Fortune. Pirates and officers alike jumped across the rails and boarded the trader. Several of the Spanish officers came out of their cabin and began to fire pistols at the pirates, wounding two of them severely. The other pirates quickly subdued the officers and tied them up.

There were only a few Spanish crewmen who were left unwounded or killed. They surrendered to the pirates. When the Spanish ship was completely subdued, Captain Roberts boarded the vessel. The Spanish captain then appeared on deck and formally surrendered to the pirates.

Roberts called the two pirates that had been wounded by the Spanish officers. He gave each of them a pistol and lined up the Spanish officers who had shot them. Bart directed the wounded pirates to shoot the officers, which they were more than happy to do. The bodies of the officers were then thrown overboard.

The blood from these men who had been shot quickly attracted several large sharks that continued to circle the two boats. The bodies of the dead Spanish crew that was killed by the splatter gun of the Fortune were then thrown overboard. The pirates got a kick out of watching the sharks devour the bodies of these men who moments before had been firing upon them.

Roberts asked the Spanish captain to show him to the treasures that they were carrying. The captain refused to do so. He said that he would surrender his ship but not the treasures thereof.

Captain Roberts stepped close to the Spanish captain as he made his way to look for the bounty. At that opportunity, the Spanish captain drew a dagger and tried to stab the pirate's captain. Before the Spaniard could get the knife fully drawn, he was hit in the shoulder by three musket balls from the onlooking pirates.

Bart turned to the pirates and told them that this assassin was theirs to do with as they pleased. The pirates took the wounded Spanish captain and tied his arms to a rope. They then slowly lowered him off the boat until his feet hit the water. The circling sharks instantaneously took notice. They swarmed to the hanging man and began fighting for who would eat his feet. A quick jerk on the rope was felt by the pirates. They lifted the Spanish captain up and found that his feet were both gone. The captain was screaming as the pirates lowered him back down for the sharks to continue their feast. Little by little they lowered the captain down until the sharks had completely devoured his entire body.

Black Bart ordered his pirates to search the entire ship and find the treasure. Boards were ripped from the below deck area and the entire living facility of the Spanish ship was totally destroyed. When the pirates returned above deck they presented their captain with several boxes of gold bullion, coins, and jewelry. They reported to him that the entire lower deck had been destroyed for them to find all the booty.

Luckily for the remaining twelve Spanish crew, there was a small life raft on their ship. It was lowered overboard, and the crewmen lowered into it. They were given some provisions and set adrift.

The pirates returned with their captain to their vessel, untied from the Alicia and drifted away. Before they had left the Spanish ship, they lit a fire down in the hold. This fire quickly spread, and the entire ship was soon ablaze.

As Fortune hoisted its sails and left the scene of this pillaging, they could see the Alicia completely engulfed in flames. They could also see the small life raft drifting off in the direction of the Canary Islands.

CHAPTER 6

When the pirates and officers were back on their own ship, Fortune, they assigned three men to count out the bounty, which they had just procured. Once the three men were sure of the total amount of ill-gotten treasures, the captain ordered that each pirate was to go to the "counting room" and receive his share of the prize.

Pirate ships, their officers, and their crew were very democratic in their dealings with one another. The captain saw to it that the men who had placed their lives on the line to overtake the opposing ship got their fair share of the bounty. Roberts knew that if he kept the crew and officers happy and content, he would have complete corporation from them when it came to manning and operating the ship.

Each sailor was given a small wooden chest, which could be locked when their treasures were placed within them. The pirates had a code of ethics that prevented other pirates from stealing their treasure chest. It was a capital offense for one pirate to steal from another. It was a more serious offense if an officer were found to have stolen from a crew member. In this manner, all aboard the ship could rest assured that their share of any bounty would stay in their possession. Of course, there were always cases where some pirate thought that he would get away with something. There was little place to run and hide. The thief would soon be found out and his fate was left to the captain and the crew, usually it was death by hanging.

The officers and the captain received their portion of the stolen bounty, which was quickly stowed away from sight. The captain also took a share for the boat itself. The captain's share was 10% of the take. Each officer received 5% and each crewman received 2%. The ship received the amount that was left over. That was usually about 40% of the treasures. The boat's share went into the coffers for the protection of the crew. They were provided with any medical attention that they may require. It also was used to pay the widow and family of any pirate who may have lost his life in serving the ship.

The captain then called a meeting of all the crew and officers. He asked them where he should direct

Fortune from there. Should they proceed to ravage trade ships or should they go back to port to enjoy debauchery and wenching? They each had plenty of monetary means to really enjoy themselves if they were to go back to port. If they went on to the trade routes of the other wealthy trade ships, they could secure more treasure, but who needed that? The pirates long term hope and desire was to live through that day and be able to sleep well that night. There were no further plans or expectations.

After a short discussion, a vote was taken. The pirates all wanted to steer directly to Port Royal, Jamaica, where they knew was the largest selection of wenches, barrooms, and rum. Black Bart swung the ship around and set his course west by southwest and directly for Jamaica.

The Atlantic crossing was uneventful. Since the trade winds were at their stern the entire way, they were able to cut two days off the sailing time. Roberts steered the ship's course to the south of Hispaniola and closely approached the southeast section of Cuba. Fortune was piloted carefully through the many small islands that lay to the south of Cuba. These islands housed many shallow reefs which had taken the lives of several ships that had tried to maneuver her channels. It was always advisable to sail this stretch of water during the daytime so that the changing depths of the waters could easily be seen. After they cleared the southern islands of Cuba, they headed directly toward the eastern end of Jamaica.

Tucked safely behind Jamaica, on the southeastern part of the Island, was the extremely active trading port of Port Royal. This port housed the largest amount of pirate booty along with the largest number of people trying to steal it from one another. To say that Port Royal was a den of corruption and debauchery was an understatement. It was much worse than anyone could imagine. Unlike Nassau, Port Royal was overrun with cutthroats and thieves. The women were ugly but plentiful and the rum flowed around the clock. A pirate was well informed to take only the money that he planned to spend. All other goods should be left on the ship where it would be carefully protected by the assigned lookouts and guards.

The lights of Port Royal could be seen aglow for many miles to sea. When approaching this port, a ship could easily see the markings of the channels and the depths of the water. There were small houses that were constructed many miles up into the local mountains. This active village also spread out laterally for 30 miles. The sounds of the Jamaican music and the smell of the burning ganga could be enjoyed by the pirates for a long distance before they were secured at the port.

Once making their way to find a berth to secure themselves to the dock and properly secure themselves to the piers, the crew of Fountain, leaving six men behind to protect the vessel, quickly found their way to completely immerse themselves in the frolicking activities of the other sailors. There were about forty ships moored to the local docks. From these, there were about 800 pirates who had been released onto the fine Port. When the other pirates found that the Fortune's men were under the command of Black Bart, they gave them a wide berth and full respect.

Captain Roberts remained on his vessel until the afternoon of the next day. He was none too anxious to see the trouble that his crew was capable of stirring up among the residents of the Port.

As was their original plans, Fortune remained moored at port for four full days. This would give the pirates of Roberts' vessel time to sober up enough to find their way back to the ship and properly sail her out into the Caribbean. As the vessel sailed away, most of her pirates lamented about the beautiful lass that they had to leave behind. Beauty was obviously in the eye of the beholder.

They sailed to the east and somewhat south of Cuba and Hispaniola, and then headed their vessel north toward Nassau, where Roberts planned to sell some of his bounty and restock the ship for more profitable activities on the high seas. Although the current ship Fortune was quite effective in battles at sea, Captain Roberts still hoped to find another vessel that was faster and carried more fire power. His only real interest was to subdue those trade ships that were laden with gold. He could easily change the name of the new ship to Fortune as he had done several times previously. The pirates were all imagining what pleasures waited for them in Nassau while Captain Bart was picturing his desires for a new vessel.

CHAPTER 7

As Fortune approached the port of Nassau, Captain Roberts sailed very close to a ship that caught his attention. This ship was almost exactly what Black Bart was looking for to replace his current ship. It was sleek and well designed to go very fast when under sail. There were 18 cannons on the port and 18 more on the starboard. She appeared to be well equipped for any type of battle that might come her way. Her name was Third rock, and Roberts could hardly wait to get to port to check on whether she was for sale.

Roberts quickly disembarked his ship when it was secured to the port's main pier. Almost in a run he proceeded to the harbor master's pavilion and inquired who was the owner of the Third rock which lay at anchor in the bay. He was directed to a local tavern where he was to ask for Captain John Roth. To the tavern Black Bart hurried without any hesitation for others along the way. He had knocked two people down before he finally reached the Wench's Dream tavern. Once inside he began inquiring about the whereabouts of one Capt. John Roth.

Captain Roth's crew did not take kindly to having someone actively searching out their leader. Roberts, because of his clothing and distinctive headwear, was known to be the captain of a pirate vessel but no one knew who he was nor what he wanted with their captain. Bart was swiftly escorted into a small back room where several sabers were placed at his throat.

"What be your interest with the man John Roth?" one of the abductors blurted out. "He fancies to speak only to those of his acquaintance and you don't be one of them."

Captain Roberts reached deep into one of his vest pockets and drew out a handful of Spanish gold doubloons.

"Tell Roth that I have some serious business to speak with him about. Tell him that I am Captain Bartholomew Roberts, better known as Black Bart. I fly the pirate colors of the Fortune and I would be pleased to make his acquaintance."

The abducting pirates released Captain Roberts and hurried off to speak with their leader, the captain of the Third rock. Very soon they returned with an invitation for Roberts to follow them to meet captain Roth. They went to an upper-level room where Roth was enjoying the presence of several wenches and some fine rum from the island of Barbados.

"Please enter Captain Roberts. I am honored to be in your company. Would you care to share some rum with me, or perhaps a wench or a cigar?" Roth blurted out.

Roberts replied that he wasn't a drinker, but he would love to have one of Roth's fine Cuban cigars. As Bart moved further into the small room, he noticed that Roth had several of his bodyguards posted close by to observe the conversation.

"Sir," began Captain Roberts. "I'm the owner of a fine sailing pirate ship. She reaches 72 feet from stem to stern, her bow spring not being included. She carries twenty-four worthy cannons that will fend off any trader on the main. I have seen the silhouette of your fine ship laying at anchor in the harbor. If you are interested, I would like to propose a trade of my ship and adequate gold loot for your worthy vessel. I would, of course, need to inspect your ship and could do so at first light tomorrow morning. I am certain that if I am satisfied with what I see, the offer I make to you will certainly be to your liking."

Captain Roth, without moving from his comfortable position between two wenches, said, "Captain Roberts, I am in love with no vessel nor with any woman. I conduct my business aboard any vessel that may be at my discretion. Meet me at 7 A.M. on the main pier and we will proceed to providing you with a disclosure of the Third rock. Plan to bring along several of your trusted crew for I would like for all details to be brought out in the open."

The next morning Roberts and Roth met as planned on the main pier. They boarded Fortune and sailed directly out to Third rock. On the way out, Captain Roberts gave Captain Roth a complete tour and disclosure of Fortune. There were four of Roth's men and four of Roberts' men who were invited on this venture of discovery. All of Roth's men were extremely impressed with the entire layout of Fortune.

When they boarded and examined Third rock, Roberts found that it was exactly what he had been wanting. After the tour was complete, all ten men met together on the above foredeck. The sale and exchange papers were drawn up and both captains were very satisfied with the transaction. The entire group sailed on the Fortune back to port. The only requirements that Captain Roberts made to Captain Roth was that he was to be permitted to remove the name Fortune from his old vessel and replace the name of Third rock on the new vessel with Fortune. This and all details were agreed upon and the transaction was complete. Captain Roberts turned over the agreed upon gold to Captain Roth, the Third rock was brought in and moored at the main pier, and the transfer of personal possessions was made from one vessel to another.

CHAPTER 8

Three days after the sale and transfer were completed for Roberts' new vessel, it sailed out of Nassau harbor and steered directly east to the area of the Atlantic where the trade ships were sure to be. The name of the new ship was changed to Fortune, like all the other ships that Roberts commanded. The crew of the new pirate ship had expanded by Roberts hiring on some extra pirates from Nassau. Adequate food, water, rum, and gunpowder were also loaded onto the new vessel.

All the sailors on Fortune were in high spirits and eager to engage with the next trade ship. Although there was a large bounty taken from the last trade ship, most of the pirates had already spent all their share of the loot on women, booze, and gambling. They were not upset at all. They just were looking forward to refilling their pockets with gold.

"One day at a time" was the philosophy of the pirates as they sailed off to put their new ship into action with any ship from England,

Spain, Portugal, or Italy. They knew that these ships would be carrying the largest treasures, which was the only thing that they were after.

Another pirate ship was encountered while the Fortune was sailing east. They came close enough to it to exchange greetings and wish each other well. The two captains knew each other from meetings in Nassau and other ports which they frequented.

As soon as Fortune reached the shipping lane of the European traders, they spotted two rather small frigates. Fortune engaged one of them and subdued it with a minimum amount of fighting. The other small boat sailed away unharmed. Roberts and his crew secured a small amount of bounty and then sailed off without harming any of the Spanish ship's crew. The pirates of the Fortune were somewhat disappointed because the encounter had been so amicable.

"Let's save our powder for a larger ship with more bounty," Roberts told his crew.

Sailing southward for two days, Fortune encountered a large Portuguese trader, Bella Donna, which appeared to be headed toward the African slave trade port in Ghana. Fortune and its crew soon realized how swiftly their ship could catch up with another vessel. The Portuguese ship was none too anxious to give up its treasures. As Roberts knew, they needed their gold for trading for slaves.

When Fortune fired a warning cannon shot across the bow of the other ship, they simply hoisted more sail and tried to outrun the pirates. Captain Bart maneuvered his ship into position and fired two volleys of five cannons each. Half of the cannons found their mark on the hull. The other steel balls tore through the sails and rigging of Bella Donna. The ship was reduced to half of its original sail capacity, and they were dealing with two large holes along their water line. Fortune remained just outside of the reach of Bella Donna's cannons. Although the Portuguese ship was requested to surrender, it continued to sail away from the pirates.

Fortune maneuvered itself back into firing position and loosed twelve cannon balls directly at the opposing ship. These cannons were fired in a volley which lasted approximately one minute. Captain Roberts was extremely pleased at the strength and accuracy of the cannons that he had recently acquired. Eleven of the twelve cannon balls found their mark directly on the gunwale of the Bella Donna, destroying five of the enemy's six active cannons on that side. The pirates positioned themselves slightly to the stern of Bella Donna and fired four more cannons, which destroyed the only remaining functional cannon on the trade ship.

As Fortune sailed closer to the enemy ship, they found that their crew were actively prepared to fire muskets and small firearms at the pirates. Fortune opened fire with two of their splatter cannons, which disabled about half of the Bella Donna's crew. The pirate ship pulled up alongside of the Portuguese ship and the pirates threw grappling hooks to the opposing ship and pulled the lines close so that the pirates could board her.

A fierce fight broke out between the crew members of the two ships. The pirates, after fighting for some twenty minutes, subdued the Portuguese crew. Captain Roberts then found it safe to board the Bella Donna and to secure a surrender from her captain.

The Portuguese captain refused to surrender his vessel. He drew his sword and headed directly toward Captain Bart. This gave the pirates due reason to open fire on the opposing captain. He was struck with eight musket balls and died immediately. Captain Roberts turned to the other officers of the Bella Donna and asked them if they would like to live and sail their ship back to their home port. The men said that they did not want to die, so Roberts commanded his men to search the vessel and remove any and all gold, silver and jewelry.

After the booty was removed from the Bella Donna, the pirates, along with their captain, reboarded their ship, released the tie lines to the other ship and drifted away. Bella Donna, under only half of her original sail, turned to due north and headed home. Fortune headed south in search of other ships to plunder. The pirates and their captain were satisfied that their new ship was sound and completely capable of engaging most any ship on the sea. Their cannons were powerful and accurate. The ship was properly equipped for fast sailing and easy maneuvering. The only variable in the equation of how functional the new Fortune would be was the quality of the crew. At this point Captain Roberts felt that he had the finest pirate crew that he could possibly have. The crew and the captain were confident in each other, which was extremely important.

Fortune, with its crew and officers, sailed away in search of more adventures. They were looking for trouble and they were certain that they would be able to find it.